I0554376

Paris
Blinks

Paris Blinks

Fifty 50-word stories set in and around Paris

Sharon Coleman

Paper Press

Oakland, CA 2016

Paris Blinks
Sharon Coleman © 2016

Un grand merci à Rosa Lane, Kimberly Satterfield, Dorty Nowak, Pamela Brenman, Clea King, GS Scott, Barbara Campbell, Carla Kandinsky, Jeanne Lupton, other members of the Green Heart Collective, Hao C. Tran, Tomas Moniz, Willy Lizarraga. Mille bisous à Doug Mathewson and Lynn Alexander, editor and publisher of Blink Ink

Cover photo by Robert A. Fischer
Author photo by Barry Ebner

Editor, artwork, and print design by Youssef Alaoui
Paper Press Books & Assoc. Publishing Co.
First Printed in Oakland, CA
978-1-878471-49-9

ISBN 10 1-878471-50-3
ISBN 13 978-1-878471-50-5

A   P   A   P   E   R

P   R   E   S   S   B   O   O   K

Contents

With a sidelong glance we see and know the whole story.

That is a Blink —

A thimbleful of words crafted carefully and spread out on an appropriately small canvas that tells us a complete tale.

– Doug Mathewson
editor of *Blink Ink*

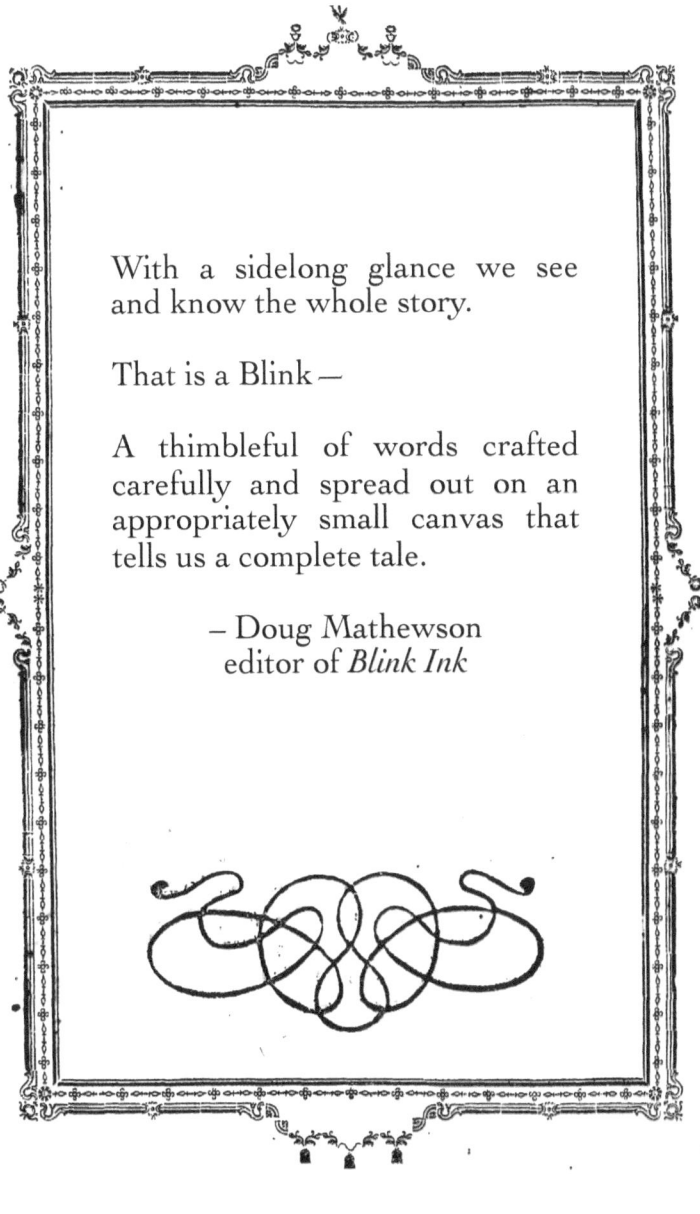

Paris
Blinks

Foreign

On a bustling Paris street, a pug struts on a leash, hits head-on something metal in a bag held by someone without a dog.

The pug is Parisian. The wrench in the bag is Parisian. The hand holding the bag is foreign. In its wrinkled stupor, the pug sees this.

Omen

She thinks it will turn out alright—this man will last
—when they stop for lunch at a small family
restaurant on the road to Paris, and a well fed tom
cat jumps on the man's lap, lifts his tail to show her
his apricot balls: fuzzy, swollen, content.

Les cris du cœur

For a hundred years, nobody replaced the curtains —torn, stained—of the abandoned psychiatric hospice near the end of the longest street in Paris. Broken windows exhale bygone cries into night. Then one spring, a commune squats, splashes graffiti and techno pop—only hashish smoke melds with the lingering old.

Close Call

They missed each other by some days. At four-thirty in the morning, in a chiffon nightdress, Astrid downed pills, walked into the lake in the *Bois de Boulogne*, drowned. Aurélie from Orléans, dressed in designer whites, settles in. France Telecom installs her new phone with, inadvertently, Astrid's now disconnected number.

G.I.

As with many war babies, Marie-Claude's history recedes as she approaches it. She found her half-brother though the Paris phonebook. But the search for her father dead-ends with an American vet with his full name but who *fought in the Pacific* and *wasn't of color*, or so his daughter says.

Metamorphosis

After a wartime childhood, "Anna Markolova" wanted to be a dancer. She took a Russian name but never grew tall enough. She teaches, collects pets, sells bric-a-brac, complains.

By sixty she wears a ratty fur coat from a long-gone paramour, accuses the concierge of harboring ex-Soviets: *Prostitutes, all of them.*

Accursed

She curses the men in the café—to deny a woman
her age. She curses them from the street under a
loose canopy of spring leaves. She curses them from
the worn curb as she lifts her greasy cotton dress.
And from the gutter as she half squats and pees.

Tender

Elizabeth gave up on her Yale dissertation but
doesn't tell anyone, not her mother the lawyer, not
the woman given to panic attacks whose children
she babysits, not the hysterical Laconian
psychoanalyst whose work Elizabeth translates.
Only her cat knows, the one who, she says, bites her
nipple at night.

Awake

After a sleepless May night preparing English lessons for French executives, Elizabeth's senses are heightened as she walks along a street of luxury apartments across from the *Bois*. She stops. Something's up. Two large green insects make love atop an iron fleur-de-lis fence post that would impale most other intruders.

Maturity

During Anouk's protracted girlhood in Bruxelles, her pink fold-up umbrella was an unlikely joy on grey days. Later under the Parisian-Lacanian gaze, it becomes a giant breast to hide behind or a billy club-phallus to clutch, menace others. Her analyst first makes her ashamed of it then desperately embrace it.

La beauté et le respect

Jae-Hwa leaves her parents' clothing business, house with the tiny pool, church, her American name in L.A., approaches Paris from the east. Frédérique serves her steak and merlot in his one-room, but the final act's fast. *Hard to give women orgasms*, he mumbles. *If I can, you can*, she frowns.

L'amour

They dine with élan, with quiet verve, with pleasure, with wine glasses filled, then emptied. They dine in love and modestly dressed as they have for forty years. If anyone notices, they would transform this roadside cafeteria by the road to Spain into a two-star bistro and travelers into lovers.

Monasticism

The monk fell in love with her paintings—gothic cathedral vaults morphing into women's bare legs. Then he loved her. When they did everything in a hotel room except penetration, he decided to be just a priest; when he found himself looking at lingerie in a store window, a historian.

Twenty-eight

She's aged, but her lovers haven't. Andreas sighs into Monique's shoe as if it were a telephone. He met her in Heidelberg—he, eighteen, studying engineering; she, thirty-six, finishing a doctorate on eroticism. He's in her Paris pied-à-terre while working a nuclear project; she's in Reims with a student.

Déjà vu

When a gypsy begging on the metro adds that she fled warring Yugoslavia, wallets open that usually wouldn't. Not Andreas Mann's... *nobody learns from our mass murder, our self-destruction....* He glimpses the gypsy, her calico skirt, remembers an almost-lover, a survivor's daughter, her bare shoulders, naked back: so vulnerable, so strong.

Le théâtre

An older man, otherwise refined they'd say, grabs the new member of the writing group by the collar, waves a fist, plays like it's a scene he's writing.

The new member deflects, describes how *quimboiseuses* from his Guadeloupe use spiritual/ practical know-how to liberate in his play. Next week neither returns.

Rue Richer et Rue Saulnier

During the Occupation, a Jewish member of the Resistance shoots a Nazi outside the *Folies Bergères*, runs down Rue Saulnier, escapes into the metro. Later he's caught, castrated during torture by the slamming of a drawer, sent to a camp. But the street's not haunted by him: he's still alive.

Produce

When news of the homegrown terrorist's arrest travels radio waves from Oklahoma to Paris, the Moroccan grocer leaves the back of his store. He grabs an orange—squeezes it as if it were the giver of life, money he doesn't have—stands in the doorway, squint-eyes tourists into buying it.

Rue Lafayette et Rue Saulnier

Transvestites shimmer by in emerald; boys anonymous in robes follow an imam; a prostitute with safety-pin piercings drinks coffee with her daughter; a woman, mistaken for a high-class whore, waits for her grandson to finish Hebrew school. And I drink beer with the only person able to guess my age.

Rue Bleue

Charles learned jazz trumpet in Tennessee, came in 1963 to Paris where he met Guillaume, who'd written a play on American football. They've lived together ever since. But on the street, you'll see them only apart. Guillaume will tell you about Charles and his play; Charles waits beneath awnings alone.

Social Inclusion

They take a break around two pm on an almost empty metro platform: two pickpockets. One French—the other African. One in a cheap, clean suit carrying a portfolio—the other jeans, empty-handed. One with six monthly metro passes—the other, one. *It's all about style. Style gets you in.*

Enforcement

The police make a show of force dragging a handcuffed Senegalese man from the Gare de Lyon. Their audience? A Hasidic man collapsing, clenching his heart. His wife shouting his soul back into him. Two Albanian girls shoved from one Fiat into another—their desperate eyes overlooked by the police.

La frontera

July 1995, bombings in Paris transform the E.U's recent open-border zones: French border police followed by machine gun-clad gendarmes fill the aisle of an Amsterdam-Paris bus. Mexican tourists gasp; a Californian expat's not surprised. Two young Frenchmen are taken. *Drugs*, their compatriot says clenching his book like a Spanish missionary.

L'arrivée

Marla anticipates her first day in a French school, imagines herself as Marie Curie in her new home. She brings flowers to the teacher, presents them with Polish pride. In the playground, she tells kids of her latest discovery: if you mix wine with sperm, you get twins. She's loved.

Inverse Proportion

On the opposite metro platform, a well-dressed couple argues, yells, almost comes to blows. On this side, a five-year-old girl watches, smiles for the first time that day. Her foreign babysitter sees the smile and, in French perfected among children, yells *Arrête!* The couple stops — as well as the smile.

Winter Circus (1)

When his hard-working father finds out, Hamid locks himself in the family apartment, watches heroin swirl down the toilet. Goes cold turkey. He thinks of Sandrine (who won't marry him) their daughter, his grandfather during Ramadan. He can't take it. Jumps from the fifth floor to get more—and lives.

Winter Circus (2)

Sandrine can't take him anymore, walks along cold streets, thinks of what Hamid had before the needles. She finds a stray dog, drags it to her mother's one-room apartment where it lives on the balcony. When it howls from cold, she lifts it by the neck, yanks hard and yells.

La liberté

A renegade Belgian journalist unemployed for an IRA interview dines in Paris with a French journalist at *L'Express*. They almost choke over Rwanda. *Belgians are pulling out* the Frenchman sneers, but he soon travels to Kigali with government officials, writes what they want written, regrets it enough to quit almost.

Surveillance

July 1995: Bomb explodes in Paris transit station.

Hot August afternoon: Two fully armed gendarmes enter a metro car, step to the back and eye a young woman: chestnut hair, low-cut t-shirt, tight jeans, baby asleep in stroller. *Are you looking for terrorists or women?* she asks. *Both* they chuckle.

L'harmonie (1)

That afternoon, Virginie goes to the *syndique* to defend her job: typing a letter for her boss, she left off the silent "h" of *harmonie*. Crossing a bridge over the Seine that evening, she peers down. The face of a suicide peers back, laughs to the cadence of vanishing letters.

L'harmonie (2)

Virginie's mother made a bridge from her young daughter's braids: one *du Gabon*, her Africa, and one *le Breton*, Virginie's northern French father. *Du Gabon et le Breton*, she tied the braids together. When he beat her, she cut them, re-coiffed her collectible dolls with their daughter's hair, left him.

L'harmonie (3)

Virginie's older sisters dance Friday evenings in their mother's Paris apartment, dance with their children as their boyfriends smoke, talk politics, soccer, Senegal. The boyfriends have even less money than Virginie's mother. Later the sisters tuck in their children three to a mattress, then fight or comb their shoulder-length hair.

L'harmonie (4)

Since he lost his job at a British cultural center in
Paris, Virginie's older brother rarely leaves his
childhood room. He sits at his child-sized desk with
Dumas and Rimbaud and the four poems he wrote.
His older sisters crumple his heart, but when
Virginie returns, he unfolds those poems.

L'harmonie (5)

Virginie won't live off her mother, whose domestic work secured a modest pension and government apartment now full with bickering children and grandchildren. Virginie earns enough for a studio on the Seine between factories and satellite dishes, but when wine runs dry, she flirts with a religious sect singing harmony.

L'harmonie (6)

In the morning, the Seine's slow brown water reflects nothing, not the smoke stacks, barges, quayside trees or trucks, just a shadow of the lowest bridge in Paris. As we gaze from her apartment window, Virginie, who tells me all her troubles, asks about mine. Only now I can't answer.

Les feuilles mortes

I ride my bike out from Paris, through the autumn leaves — my skirt flaps in the warm wind like pages written by philosophers who recently took their lives, one by the window, the other no one was told how — their remains, dying leaves that will only come alive by reading.

La politesse

As Thao waits in a park, a man trips over Thao's foot. *The French never apologize* — Thao pictures shamefaced buddies in Saigon. After the perfunctory *Pardon,* he shakes Thao's hand, dusts off his pants. Thao later respects this man's artistry — courtesy — for stealing cash from his wallet, leaving everything else.

Disdain

When the French journalist doesn't object to his American wife's shoplifting, their au pair sees it as disdain. He doesn't even shield their children from her habit. That night, the au pair contemplates a handbag the wife gave her, later leaves her lover, who also liberally helps himself to things.

La monnaie

Because he plays money games, François's friends call him *Little Jew*. When he dates a real one, they laugh. An outing in Rouen: these lovers pass Rue aux Juifs then Rue du Massacre. He laughs. That night in Paris, she turns away. He throws coins at her, slams the door.

Élan vital

After the divorce, Matilde moves to Paris to be happy. It's not easy. She tries swimming. When she steps past showers to the pool, men put their sudsy hands down their trunks. She inhales, dives. After weeks of evening swims, she walks like Aphrodite, and the men take no notice.

Le réel

Félice doesn't like Paris—so expensive compared to Strasbourg. Her husband loves it. Loves driving American babysitters home blasting rock music even though they only slam his car door. *Maybe tomorrow.* He returns to his little sons: Didier's hitched up Thibaut's legs, pretends to fuck him. They laugh and laugh.

La maternité

When Marie-Claire doesn't conceive, she adopts an Afro-Brazilian boy. When the boy turns five, he begs her to divorce. *No*, she decides. Each night, he wraps himself in an indigo cloth with patterns of migrating birds, sleeps at her door. Marie-Claire sends the nanny back to Mali, panics into motherhood.

Les parents pénibles

When Marie-Claire does conceive, she fears the baby won't be right, asks the doctor to take it, if so. The daughter arrives perfect.

Marie-Claire's husband fears the adopted boy will be jealous. It's sibling love: the baby's sticky lips always smile for the pudgy, open arms of her dark-skinned brother.

Strangers

Marie-Claire tries to befriend her husband's female friends—to avoid jealousy. He snickers at her attempts at English and mothering. But when she invites a Chinese couple and an American Jew to Christmas dinner, he—who travels Asia selling French cigarettes—good-naturedly announces "donkey" for dinner. *No. Turkey,* she corrects.

Cachet

Due to the gift's cachet, the diplomat's wife displays the mounted Buddha head in their Paris apartment. She even tries to reproduce its calm smile in her paintings. But as their son grows mentally unstable, its lowered eyes haunt them. When their son O.D.s, the diplomat repatriates the severed head.

L'imaginaire

A government official panics when a Romanian woman falls right outside his apartment door. He dreams his cheeks sink, hollow out, face disappears after bribes from a Portuguese businessman are exposed. He delays buying a summerhouse, hires a homeless man to keep watch from the street, but he disappears too.

Sans domicile fixe

Monsieur Picard didn't choose to live without a
fixed residence or to stop buying cigarettes, but he
has since rediscovered how it feels to breathe. That's
why he's leaving the new job: playing the
neighborhood bum outside the apartment of a high
government official in the grimy air of Paris.

La mort

After her mother dies in Belfast traffic, Adelaide turns Goth, rubs ash around her eyes daily. She takes up anthropology (her therapist's suggestion), studies various cemeteries, vows to spend the night in Paris's Père Lachaise amongst the famous dead. Once she's there, ghosts rise and beg to attend her wedding.

Divine Compassion

Traversing the catacombs, Yannick realizes she was a blacksmith in 1643. Gilles suffered since childhood knowing he'd been a countess locked in a donjon. They meet at a seminar at the experimental university of Paris. Together sipping vending machine coffee that stains their teeth, she offers to pick his locks.

Enlightenment

In a Left Bank teashop sit two couples. A sixteen-year-old daughter of immigrants talks passionately about Camus. She twists in her secondhand jeans as an awkward Frenchman listens, in love. A bourgeois couple sneers: *We produce new philosophers every year* as if to enlighten me, who reads Virginia Woolf alone.

Acknowledgments

Ambush Review
"Monasticism," "Cachet," "Sans domicile fixe," "Maturity," "Les feuilles mortes," "Rue Bleue," "Rue Richer et Rue Saulnier," "Rue Lafayette et Rue Saulnier," "Tender," "Awake."

Blink Ink
"Foreign," "Twenty-eight," "Le réel," "Inverse Proportion."

Lily Literary Review
"Metamorphosis."

Midway Journal
"Déjà vu."

Out of Our
"Accursed," "Produce," "Social Inclusion," "Surveillance," "Omen."

Poetry Flash
"La politesse," "Divine Compassion," "G.I.," "La mort."

Saturday Night Special Anthology
"Les cris du cœur."

Sharon Coleman is a fifth-generation Northern Californian with a penchant for learning languages and their entangled word roots.

Her poetry and short fiction have appeared in *Ambush Review, Clade Song, Rivet, Tule Review, Berkeley Poetry Review,* and her chapbook *Half Circle*; published in 2013. She writes for *Poetry Flash* and teaches at Berkeley City College.

Sharon co-curates the reading series Lyrics & Dirges and co-directs the Berkeley Poetry Festival. Her blink fictions were nominated twice for a Pushcart and once for a Micro Award.

Paper Press Books
& Associates Publishing Company is a small-scale
independent press begun in 2012 with headquarters
in both the Bay Area and the Central Coast of
California.

More
Paper Press
Books

paperpressbooks.tumblr.com

www.ingramcontent.com/pod-product-compliance
Lightning Source LLC
Chambersburg PA
CBHW050906180626
46814CB00007B/2922